Etched

Lauren Federico

Acknowledgements

Thank you to Heather and Steve. You both inspire me daily.

I also want to express my appreciation to Belinda and Alex. I am grateful for all your support.

Table of Contents

Part One

Enchanted

I am compassionate, harmonious, and sensitive.

I am flower buds floating along the river.

I am nurturing, powerful and abundant.

I am a garden growing beautiful things.

I am honest, passionate, and artistic.

I am an art gallery questioning your thoughts and perspective.

I am an innocent morning, and a wild night.

I am made of magic.

Weather

My moods are nature:

When I am mysterious or complacent,

I am a black starry night.

And when I am spontaneous or adventurous,

I am the abundant mountains.

And when I am vibrant and new,

I am the morning sunrise.

And when I am engaged or indulged,

I am the deep ocean.

And when I am curious or wondering,

I am the mystical forest.

And I change with the seasons, too.

Glimpse

I am rare.

I am a sunshower with atypical purity.

I am a blue moon with uncommon authenticity.

I am a total solar eclipse with unusual empathetic
nature.

I am a four-leaf clover with unconventional
uniqueness,

and I am the déjà vu you'll feel when you can't
forget me,

because I am the only one.

Delicate

I am sensitive,

like a rose that only blooms in better weather.

I am in tune,

the way nature harmonizes like a symphony

together.

I am passionate,

like a sunset drive.

I am divine,

like the beginning of time.

I am intricate,

like emotion.

I am deep,

like the ocean.

I am serene,

like a pause in a busy afternoon.

And I am loving,

like the definition, too.

Shades

Every day I am a new version of myself.
I have gone through phases of
reclusiveness, enthusiasm, and complacency.
I share myself with the universe through moods.
I connect with existence through state of mind.
I am emotive
and I love myself through every shade.

Mad Love

And after I've let out many works of art,
it redefines the chemistry of my body.
Its therapeutic nature heals me.
I am purely in love.
I don't create art,
art creates me.

My Magic Is Chaotic

Emotion…

You and I are in motion.

Will we make this work?

I can only hope you don't see my flaws and imperfections, and would they make you want to turn away?

Maybe you want someone who feels a little less deeply than I do, someone who feels a little less intimately about being alive.

Maybe my magic is too broad for you. Maybe my

chaos is too incredible for you.

Can I trust a soul who looks as perfect as you?

Magic is chaotic- it's beautiful, mysterious, and

unknown.

It's an imperfect mess.

And can you handle it?

Gem

I need some inspiration,

will you be the one?

You can be my moonstone

and we can begin this new connection.

Can I trust you to empower me?

When I'm down, will you comfort me?

Together, we could succeed.

Bring the good vibrations,

because I need a little magic today,

a little positive energy.

Constellation

Late night thoughts…
What's on your mind?
We can talk about anything,
no expectations or judgement,
just truth.
We can express our connection
and go to the place the universe takes us
when we're alone together.
Our souls can't lie.
Let's be honest with ourselves,
then we will glow like the stars.

Simplicity

You move the hair away from my face
and I look up at you, wide-eyed and quiet.
Conversation is extraordinary,
but nothing is better than comfortable silence.

Drawn

I am quiet, like the gentle oncoming of the
morning,
when I find you through the night to feel our
connection.
I don't say so, but you make me feel awake and
brand new.
I'm as sure of you as the promising sunrise.
Your existence captivates me how time attracts
light.
I wonder who you are.

Sky Blue

Blue is the color I feel when you're with me.

My mind is a kaleidoscope of aquas and deep

blues.

Nothing is as free as sky blue,

or me when I'm with you.

Ocean blue is when

we are indulged in the moment:

detail, consistency, depth, time.

Indigo is when I am indulged in you:

stories untold, comfortable silence, conversation

without words, our secrets within the truth.

Turquoise is the trust I'm growing into

with you…

I let go.

High

I fell in love with you the way the trees grow
toward the sun:

I grew from your energy,
and you took me to the sky.

In Your Atmosphere

Being with you is like being in the sun after an
eternity of shade.
Being near you feels like being in the light for the
first time.
You nurture me like the sun to its flowers.
You grow me through love.
That is why I want to expose every part of myself
to you- every part of my mind, body, heart, and
soul.
That is why I want you to see the deepest parts of
me,
because I feel enlightened when you touch me.

Florescence

It was springtime next to you,

and I was in bloom

like a wildflower field,

growing through you.

You always made me feel so beautiful and

limitless,

as you held me in your dark room.

Your eyes never left mine,

those tranquil nights,

when I gently blossomed

for you.

Art Is Subjective

Oh, how original it was for you
to create a masterpiece of me through your
perception.
I felt impassioned to be your muse
and let your love define me.
I was a blank canvas
and your eyes were paint.
I was art in your vision.
Now I'm pouring you out through words
onto the page
because I, too, am inspired.

Perfection

Your palm holds my face,

and your thumb caresses my cheek,

as though I am delicate.

I am vulnerable with you.

Your eyes don't ask permission to witness my soul.

I smile and breathe you in.

Your undivided attention intoxicates me.

You are intrigued by me, and I am fascinated by

you.

I am lost in desire for you.

Perception

Being with you was weightless-

like we were two birds, drifting.

I felt your every movement inside of my soul.

You inspired me.

I broke for you.

It was a beautiful scene, being in your perception.

I healed within our silent eye contact.

I fell in love under your gaze.

It was when we were breathing the same breath

that we were connected.

Dizzy

The moon switched shifts with the sun,

but time stood still.

Together, we watched the world spin that evening.

I remember the dim blue oncoming night

and every detail of your smile

and the lines under your eyes.

It's engraved in my mind.

All I knew was your presence next to me

and thinking,

"How can someone make me this

happy?"

You stayed with me from sunset to sunrise.

I remember the way the early morning

sunrays beamed through the window as you said

you had to go.

You were my best friend at the time

and 5 am seemed like an eternity without you.

You smiled down at me…

The truth behind your smile remains unknown.

2013

The hum of your car down the road made me
drowsier than 2 am. My sleepy eyes were weighing
heavy as we left the party and floated along the
back roads toward town. You looked over at me
and smiled. "We're almost home," you assured me,
as your hand caressed the back of my neck. But all
I needed was your voice to get me there. Just you.

Croghan Street

Every time I hear that song,
I am back in your dad's living room
wasting the day away,
singing tunes.
We always found time for music,
like that day we listened to that random mixtape
we found on the floor in your room
and related on that same song.
I still hear that summer heat
and cloudy afternoon.
We always connected through music,
but we didn't know it when we first met.
We had both come from a background of it
and it's where we both ended up:
connecting through art
and singing together on a Friday night.

How these memories are irreplaceable in my soul.

More Than Friends

You're beautiful, honey.

You walk around unnoticing.

You keep a firm grasp on your control over
everything,

but you don't see how incredible you are

when you just let go,

so let go.

And maybe you'll see yourself in the same light I
see you in,

look into the mirror and see a flawless reflection.

But you and I are a story untold.

Still, I hold our memories close

of the days when we were

in the same places.

Now, you're always on the go,

searching for the missing pieces.

I hope you find all that you wanted,

and maybe you'll remember me.

Lucid

I kept it a secret

to keep the peace between us,

but it only poisoned the peace within me.

It has been two years since you said

you felt something for me too,

back when I was sitting in my car alone that night.

The moonlight shone through the darkness

like your words.

It still relaxes me to know you felt the same

even though you've been away

and the days go by.

Now tell me, darling,

how do I let you go?

Echo

It's easy to admire beginnings.

They are new and exciting:

the innocent first dates, the gentle exchange of the first few smiles, the beauty of a new connection.

Beginnings are something special and worthwhile.

But what about endings?

The pain I feel from your absence is just an echo of the peace I felt in your presence.

And that, too, is beautiful.

Part Two

August Rain

And so it goes:

another day in the rain.

More clouds, doom, and downfall from the sky.

The sky is falling!

The raindrops pelt the ground to spite your

absence.

Another day after you.

You are the end of a chapter in a book that I am

unable to go back and reread on rainy days.

You are the stiffness in my bones the weather

change always brings.

I am aching for the sunlight,

aching for daybreak,

aching for your love to come find me again.

Only for a Moment

I want to stop feeling for you. I want to undo the
time we were driving back from the park, and you
made me laugh so hard I almost cried. The sky was
a dim blue, and the sun was setting in the rearview.
I want to rewind the band at the winery and redo
the day we went to the festival and visited the
antique shop downtown. You let me walk in front
of you so you could watch me walk. Your
complete attention was always on me. Your eyes
never left me. What about the days when you knew
what I was thinking? You practically read my mind
most of the time. I want to reset all the good
morning and good night messages, and all the days
on end we spent together. I want to forget the
comfortable silence and gazes in the darkness, how
your eyes always found mine, and how they
thought my every move was beautiful. I want to let
go of feeling your hands in my hair, how we
helped each other grow, and the way your mind
brought me peace. I want to take back letting
myself fall. I want to stop feeling for you,

because I feel numb without you.

Reminisce

"You always look so pretty in the morning," you
said, as you looked down at me,
and I looked away.
You were looking for sustenance,
and instead, you found me.
But that time in our lives was just an autumn leaf
that blew into December.
I hope you think of me on Sundays,
like the day I asked you what you wanted
and you said, "you."
I hope you remember me when you hear
alternative rock music.
I hope it makes you happy to reminisce
my delicate nature,
the way I was art,
and how deeply passionate I felt about life.
These poems are words I could never relay,
free verses that won't change a thing.

Without You

Nothing can compare to how normal things felt
when we were together.
Our souls were completely in sync
with one another.
Our connection was undeniable and
stood out in the room.
I was so accustomed to you being around me,
so comfortable with my life with you.
We listened to the same music,
hung out with the same crowd
at the same places,
trusted the same universe,
breathed at the same pace...
It feels so unnatural without you.
I'm still learning how to be myself without you.
Some days it feels like something's missing- or
everything-
an empty space I can't fill,

without you.

Part of Me

You were always unapologetically yourself,

someone I could never forget

or live without.

But your ghost hangs around me now

filling the void where you used to be.

Is that weird?

Because you're gone,

but I know you well enough to know what you're

thinking.

You've got everything under control now,

and how does it feel?

Timing is hard to get right

but I've always felt you unlike anyone else,

and you're a part of me.

I never let it show.

Still, I remember all your art

that you have tattooed on your body now.

I miss your smile

and my lifestyle of denial
with you.

Through Your Eyes

Sometimes I still see myself

through your eyes,

like the way you'd tell me I look like my mom,

or how you like my hair black,

or those days in high school when you would drag

me out of my room when I was depressed.

Now all we have is time

keeping us distanced.

I wonder how much of it

you will let go by.

I look back and regret not appreciating the time we

had together more,

but what does anyone know at 17?

I can still feel you some days

and I wonder if you still feel me,

because when I lost you,

it feels like I lost a part of me.

Now I'm wondering what you see.

Pieces

My hair has grown out since the last time I saw
you.

It's been years since you've been home.

A few messages here and there don't add up to
much.

The distance between us is piercing during the day
when I'm alone,

and I wonder how you spend your time

and if you're happy.

I heat another cup of tea

and pour my emotions onto the page.

I guess working things out is out of the question.

I thought you read my eyes when they

said,

"Don't ever leave me."

Now I'm the air you'll never breathe.

People usually say that your head and your heart
disagree,

but I don't see it so black and white.

Even though you couldn't stay,

in some way,

we were eternal.

I still carry pieces of you with me.

I wonder if you carry pieces of me, too.

10 Years

Did you forget me?

Since you left town, I haven't slept in months.

Do you still think of me?

I always found my way to you in high school

when we were young.

You were so charismatic,

and I was shy.

Things were changing around us

but I never changed my mind

about you.

You decided it wasn't right between us

and I pretended like that was fine.

Now I'm pacing through the fallen leaves

in Ohio

and thinking about that year we spent every day

together.

You were always my best friend, honey.

Our conversations are shortening like the daylight,

and I'd give anything for one more minute of your time.

Dream

I had you, then I lost you.

Just like that, you were gone.

I didn't know that would be the last time,

that morning I awoke to feelings of dismay.

Like a yin and yang,

you brought black to my spotless white,

shadows to my light,

bitterness to my lemonade,

and chaos to my fairy-tale scene

when you disrupted my sleep.

Now from this dream,

I must awake.

But your selfishness was alright.

I'll ignore this disdain.

I'm just a bird flying to you,

but I've lost sight of you, anyway.

Comfortably Quiet

I don't tell you how I feel because...

You like blonde hair and mine is black.

I'm a peachy sunset and you're the nightlife downtown.

You're always making sure your needs are met and I'm always helping others.

I'm strongly opinionated, and you're reserved and collected.

You like cats but I'm allergic.

I like plants but you hate the clutter.

I dread the snow, but you love the changing seasons.

We are worlds apart,

so, I stay comfortably quiet.

Alternative Playlist

Acceptance is realizing

that everything is the way it's meant to be

and the truth isn't worth fighting,

but how you were with me was so gratifying.

Your smile was contagious,

what a beautiful lie.

I wish you weren't fake,

and I could believe the mask you hide your chaos

behind.

I'm wishing you were really sorry.

I keep reliving last fall

when I was away with my family,

and you sent me a playlist

full of songs on it about a girl

who was only being loved halfway,

but she stayed anyway.

I should have seen the sign of the times.

Discontinued

I wonder if you remember me when the seasons change, like that fall when we first met. We were young, but I knew then that I wanted you. I remember that summer when we fell asleep together in the camper. It felt safe to sleep next to you. I remember that winter after, you kissed me for the first time. I still haven't looked at snow the same since. Despite our bittersweet days, I knew you wouldn't stay.

Nicotine

You and a pack of cigarettes have a lot in common.

Your presence is short-lived and cheap.

Yet, you've hooked me, and now you are a bad
habit of mine.

You're harmful and toxic to my body.

You're cunning and deceptive to my mind.

Yet, I am dependent on your benefit.

I crave your effect.

Withdrawal sets in when you're not around.

I am addicted.

I Stopped Counting the Days

It's been seven months
and you finally came around,
but it doesn't matter now,
because your lies permeated me.
You're responsible for this casualty
and I'm emotional at best.
I wish you could see just what you've done,
the way I've seen so many shades of you-
colors of who you are.
Now I'm writing pages of you
because your presence left a mark.
Being with you was metamorphic.
I can still see your reflection in my surroundings.
I still want you, even though you repel me
because we could never reach common ground.

Distance

You inspire me.
Oh, what I would do
to waste my time with you
for one more day.
We don't talk but
your goodbyes aren't promising.
Every time you left
you didn't have to feel the pain
of being caught in the in-between.
Did you think I wouldn't mind?
Now you're always with me
because I bring you back every time I write.
I keep asking myself when this will end,
this idea of you in my head?
And everything you've ever said?
And how do I say goodbye?

Swayed

6 am.

The early March sunrise was taking its time
as my body ached from sleeping on the floor with
you that night.

You got so drunk.

Your selfish decisions are hard to forget.

"Stay with me tonight, baby."

The truth is, I just couldn't wait to leave the bar.

Coming to terms with the past now, I see how you
swayed me.

I was always nervous and had to fake it,

but I used to love who I was when I was with you.

My window was hazy in the rearview from the rain
as I left that morning,

the drawn-out hours of the night peering through
me,

and your desolate eyes.

You always came around to waste my time.

Delphinium

Illusion- you appear innocent, beautiful, inviting…

but you infect the ones you touch.

How can you be so alluring yet so untrue?

Many approach you, but only few survive you.

How can you be so appealing, yet so dangerous?

Sweet, deceptive existence…

This attraction is fatal.

You send my head spinning.

You paralyze me.

Honey, you are a delphinium flower.

Shadow

I wonder if you have any regrets

or if you think of me throughout your day.

Do you see my face in the passengers you drive by

on the streets?

Or do you hear me in the songs on the playlist you

replay?

Do you find me through conversations with

strangers you meet?

Or in scenes of the movies you see?

Do I cross your mind when you're on your own

late at night, alone?

Does your body ache for me?

Or do you erase me with every attempt to avoid?

Pause

I know I come to mind

when you're on your way to work

in the morning,

and the red light stalls your schedule,

your coffee steams a little longer than usual,

your phone is unexpectedly silent,

and there are moments in your routine

that give you time to think of me.

Part Three

Sparse

You were the partly cloudy days
in the summertime.
You were a shadowed moon phase
dimming the night.
You were a fire that burned
for only a short amount of time.
You were the candle
that refused to light.

Car Wash

The last time I saw you, we drove past that car wash in our hometown that we stopped at in high school once or twice. That was the night you blamed your job that you were on the road for on why we could never make it. It was always an excuse with you, never the truth. My chest collapsed as we turned the corner of that car wash, my body aching, my pain silently filling your truck. I know you felt my heart break.

That was the last time.

Memory

The deeper I let myself feel,

the more deeply I feel you,

but I wish it were you making me come alive

instead of feeling everything alone.

Now that you're gone,

you're a hunger I will never quite satisfy,

a void I will never fill.

Sometimes it feels like you died,

but you've always lived on the other side.

When you left,

it was like you were never a part of it all,

but you were the only one there when I was alone.

It was just you and I.

Even though you were toxic,

I can't forget how close you were to me-

skin to skin, soul to soul.

Even though you were hurting me,

I miss feeling you close to me at all.

Fatal Attraction

I passed that house today,

the place where I first saw you.

I touched the mailbox.

You walked by again

in my memory,

and our eyes met:

our first moment of intimacy…

But the silence between us was suffocating

and I'd held my breath ever since,

or was that your hand across my face?

Reservoir

The depression lives in my bones,

the anxiety under my skin.

My body aches in all the places I let you in,

and you flood my mind again.

I am the levee containing you all day,

but at night, I break,

and you flow through me,

filling all the empty space.

Karmic Relationship

Thank you for making me strong.
I will always live with your soul in the palm of my
hand.
I sold my soul to believe in you,
and lost it all when I turned to find you were
unattainable.
You set me ablaze when you were done with me.
The fire is still burning through my veins.
You corrupted me until I was no longer myself,
just something you poisoned with your touch.
Now my soul is a blown-out candle,
smoking…
I lost myself searching for you.
I would give anything to feel something other than
this numbness
and clouded senses…
…can't even see where you are anymore.
I always knew it would be you crossing me.

Forbidden

I dream of snakes whenever you come near me.
Your eyes tell white lies as you awake in the
morning.
You've convinced me that these things take time,
that day after day, I'll wait and wait
for you to come closer and be mine
but I never stopped waiting.
Another bottle of Moscato emptied.
Another rock album overplayed,
but I listen to the same songs over and over again
to drown out my madness
and the little voice that says
you dim my light.

Ghost

I found the feeling I have been chasing and running
from:
You slept all day, you would never wake up.
You never knew who I was.
You were incapable of love.
I still search for a reason
why you would vandalize my identity
and disavow the repercussions of your actions.
I still save myself from you every day.
I've given up everything to change.
Now we both feel your pain,
but some days I can't feel anything at all.

Inhibited

With every exhale, I silently release you.

It was always your voice in my ear telling me I was
nothing.

It was always you standing behind me as I looked
into a shattered mirror.

Your abuse spread through me like a disease.

So many nights that I lost sleep.

You were made of empty promises and hollow
kindness.

You disrupted me, endlessly.

Disown

Your vain decisions always distressed me.
Being with you was like
being alone at a party
full of lively people, laughing and having fun.
You always disowned me,
even when I was standing next to you,
because it was your world,
I was just living in it.

Disguised

He said, "You're so sure of yourself,"

cognizant, casual, and composed.

I wondered if it was easy to fake that kind of

magnetism.

I brushed off the half-compliment and tried to

appreciate the night,

but it's wearing to look into eyes that lie.

Narcissist

Sweet. Devoted. Interested. Sincere. Inspiring. Lovely…

…Contradictory. Entitled. Secretive. Threatening. Pervasive…

Innocent. Kindhearted. Loyal. Empathetic…

…Controlling. Manipulative. Deceptive…

…Unpredictable. Dissociated. Absent. Abuser.

Different

I am

the first glimpse of the morning sunrise,

and you are

the middle of a somber black night.

I am everything you're not,

and we are unalike.

Deception

I deserved love,

when you gave me absence.

But I am worth everything you neglected to give,

and more.

Depression

Numb. Empty. Dark. Mundane. Dull. Colorless.
Tiring. Lonely. Desperate. Hopeless. Quiet. Still.
Silent. Low. Discontent. Absent. Cold.
Disconnected. Anxiety. Mood swings. Tension.
Stress. Fatigue. Agitation. Trauma. Pain.
Disruptive. Strange. Preventive. Inconvenient.
Dysfunctional. Liar. Sadness. Destructive. Twisted.
Stuck. Pointless. Worthless. Disdain. Clinical.
Disorder. Illness. Messy. Inconsistent. Struggle.
Avoidant. Gloomy. Thief.

Body Dysmorphic Disorder

Should I leave the house today?

I've changed my clothes twelve times.

Yesterday I thought I looked alright.

Today my shoulders are too broad.

My waist is too small.

Has my nose always looked like that on my face?

I *need* a new hairstyle.

I feel fat.

Am I disproportionate?

I look too skinny.

Is there something wrong with my size?

…I'm not going.

Anxiety

Fear...

of abandonment and commitment.

of absence and consistency.

of the past and the future.

of you and myself.

of stagnation and time moving on.

of staying the same and changing.

of lies and the truth.

of denial and acceptance.

Paper Cuts

You grazed me…

…every time you refused accountability.

…with every act of denial.

…every time you failed to consider me.

…with every change you didn't make.

Now my body is filled with paper cuts
and you're to blame.

Trauma

I'm comfortable with selfish love

because that's all I'm used to.

Life has taught me

that I have to sacrifice my boundaries to be loved,

that my life is a battlefield for others' satisfaction,

that somehow, I am not enough.

Now "healthy" seems far-fetched,

"normal" feels too out of reach,

and anxiety is my natural state.

Though converting is otherworldly and unknown,

I have to grow.

I am still getting comfortable with "normal."

Boundaryless

You were a red flag I let slide.
You were a secret I had to hide-
the truth from myself to stay close,
but I only denied myself, for you,
every time I didn't say no.

Imposter

If I had the chance to say hello to you,

I wouldn't.

I would just pass you by

like the strangers we've become.

Separate

I'm lonely like the raindrops coursing down my
window:
they race each other to the ledge,
but they never meet.

Unforgotten

On hard days,

I play that record you bought me

and after it's played through,

I set it back down on my shelf

next to the memory of you.

Stranger

Maybe in a better time and place
we could be,
but we are both on our own paths
to self-discovery.

So, I choose to ignore you.

Energy

I spite you with every word that I write,
and despite you, I've written a book.

Part Four

The Little Things

Intimacy:

it's the first sip of coffee in the morning.

it's the new leaf on your favorite plant.

it's the song you listen to on repeat in the car.

it's the happiness you feel when things in life begin
falling together.

it's the scrunch your face makes when you break
down alone and cry.

it's found in the road less traveled by and in the life
of the party.

it's the most popular secret.

it's trusting the universe to hold you.

it's feeling close- close to existence.

Etched

Life is a collection of many measureless moments
that impact us.

Enough

It is a deep tragedy to ever believe

that love has to hurt,

that we deserve to only be half-loved,

or loved only on occasion,

that somehow love is conditional,

that we either earn it or we don't,

that we are not already created in it,

that there is not evidence of love in our every
gesture,

that it is not obvious that we are made of pure love
itself.

Disposition

We don't get to determine who we care about in
life,
some people just stir us deeply on the inside.

Cosmic

Our timing aligned the way
the moon meets the sun in a solar eclipse:
briefly- only for a moment.

Then we parted ways
and continued along our journey
we were destined to
by the universe.

Growing Experience

Our experiences shape us into who we are. There are some moments with you that I wish I could keep, but time changes things. Remembering the days we spent together, you showed me that it was okay. You changed my perspective, and you helped me to love myself. Even though you're gone, I still carry parts of you with me. Life is not the same since I met you. I grew through my experiences with you. You are the reason for the poems.

Out of the Woods

To everyone who helped me along the way:

thank you for being my friend in a time of

darkness,

for being the light at the end of my tunnel,

for being you.

You let the sun shine through the trees

when I could see no light at all.

You helped guide me home.

Thank you for helping me find my way.

Trust

The best relationships in life are defined by love,
not labels.

Soulmate

You know you love someone…

when you always care how they are doing.

when you'd give anything for them to feel happy.

when you always want them there with you in the moment.

when they feel important to your own well-being.

when they change you on the inside.

Best Friend

A best friend is a family member that you choose,

someone who always empathizes with you,

someone who loves you, unconditionally,

someone who has seen you in all your ways and

still chooses to stay,

someone who is with you, always,

someone who you connect on all your deepest pain

with,

someone you want to be there on all the best days

of your life,

someone you grow with,

someone you never plan to lose,

someone in all your favorite memories,

someone you share secrets with,

a home that always calls you back.

Stay

When we collide,

he will listen to me speak.

he will be compassionate, empathetic, and kind.

he will care about how he makes me feel.

he will share his emotions and communicate his
thoughts with me.

he will acknowledge my heart and mind and how
they are beautiful.

he will prioritize me.

he will help me love myself because he loves me.

And he will stay.

Intuition

Intuition is an eye
that sees
where we are not looking,
our silent guide.

It is the rhythm of our souls,
a whisper we trust.
It is a truth we are born with,
the deepest part of us.

Masterpiece

Art allows us to access the deepest parts of our
emotions,
and creates something extraordinary from the
chaos.

Free-Spirited

Passion is a gift from creation:

It breaks us deep on the inside.

It gives us a reason, a purpose.

Our passion is our truth:

It tells a story about who we really are.

It is a part of our identity.

It defines us.

Our passion is the air we breathe:

We don't go a day without.

It brings color to a world in shades of grey.

It helps us expand our understanding about life.

Passion sets us free, infinitely and eternally.

Ohio July

Driving with the windows down,

it is still light out at 9 pm.

The air is still warm

while the golden sunset eventually burns out,

and the purplish-pink sky sleeps.

Fireflies flicker and locusts hum

to accompany the twilight.

A free-spirited breeze passes through the trees

and we are awake.

Now, the indigo night sky

is illuminated with dotted fluorescence,

and clarity,

by stars that guide us in the dark.

In the distance, fireworks shoot and pop-

the kind you lightly feel in your chest.

Smoke dissipates into the atmosphere from the

burning light

and sparks fly.

Summer nights live on forever.

Lime Street

Still nights were assisted by sounds of train wheels
on the tracks,
where I grew through shades of self-discovery
and changed with the Ohio seasons, too.
Rainy Aprils filled our uneven driveway with
puddles,
and sunny Julys brought shade from trees in our
back yard,
where we felt the earth under our bare feet
and were greeted by music from the tavern
around the block
on a small-town side street called Lime.

Jade

Humans are distinctive.
We are all just like potted plants,
growing at different paces,
with separate needs.
We thrive in certain conditions,
and need consistency to grow.
We are unique,
and it is pointless to compare
one plant to another.

Human

Sensitive. Sophisticated. Intricate. Distinctive.
Knowledgeable. Adaptive. Emotional. Symmetry.
Purposeful. Divine. Compassionate. Joyous.
Natural. Progressed. Unique. Loving.

Diversity

Diversity makes us unique.
Without it,
there would be no
individuality or originality,
no room for growth or change.
Our differences are what
make us beautiful.

Lucent

We burn like the stars,
so profound and bright,
and emit our light
as we shed ourselves like stardust
throughout our lives.
And on a clear night,
we admire the beauty
of the celestial sight,
but never stop to see our own.

Glow

It's better to…

…stand rather than blend in with the crowd.

…be unique rather than basic.

…say no when you really want to.

…choose what is good over what is popular.

…be comfortable with yourself rather than
being confined by society's standards.

…be unapologetically yourself instead of being
someone else.

Caged

Let me out!

My soul is wild and free, reckless and untamed.

This cage can't keep me contained.

The ground won't define me as flightless.

Let me out!

Society can't silence me.

I am an open mouth ready to speak; hear me!

I am art on the page.

Let me out!

I have spent years battling emptiness,

going through the motions and keeping a straight
face,

longing for something true on the inside.

Let me out!

I'll dance with butterflies

and spark fire with every touch of my fingertips.
I'll find magic in the madness.

Let me out!
So I can breathe.

Woman

Independent. Resilient. Capable. Spiritual.
Intrinsic. Open-minded. Devoted. Good-natured.
Empowered. Nurturing. Intuitive. Deserving.
Strong-willed. Witty. Sensible. Pure. Exquisite.
Valid. Brilliant. Instinctive. Adaptive. Immaculate.
Equal. Human.

Curiosity

I want to know what is after pushing past my
farthest limits, beyond my comfort zone.
I'm tempted toward the life I desire.
I'm interested in the version of myself God created
me to become.
I'm drawn to my wildest dreams.
I'm attracted to the connection within myself.
I am determined to grow in love, purpose, faith,
and devotion with the universe.

Empty Fear

I used to…
sell myself short.
settle for less than I deserved.
not know my worth.

I feared…
moving forward.
letting go of the comfortable life I'd known.
changing for the better.

Because "what-if…"
change was out of my reach?
happiness was only hypothetical?
peace was unattainable?
But now, years later, I am…
ahead in my life.
mentally and emotionally strong.
content, happy, and at peace.

Don't let empty fear keep you from moving on to the life that's calling you.

Healed

Growing has become my biggest mission-

my obsession,

my candlelight in the dark,

because I used to give love away until I was empty

to those who didn't value me.

But I'm proud of who I've become

because she doesn't live there anymore.

The past is a closed door.

Feel

One of the bravest things we will ever do
is acknowledge our trauma and heal from the pain.

Worth It

Walking away from things
that didn't agree with me
is the best decision
I have ever made for myself.
Self-respect
is a priority.

Internal Wisdom

You find your strength
when you come to realize
it has always been you
who was coming through for you.

Strength

Every decision in life involves pain, so choose
positivity.

Mindful

It is worthwhile to be…

appreciative instead of mindless.
modest instead of boastful.
honest instead of avoidant.
humble instead of prideful.
empathetic instead of apathetic.

Free

Compassion is essential to happiness.

Forgive mishap

and fill in the empty space with clemency.

Offer empathy

and live free.

About the Author

Lauren Federico has been writing all throughout her life. The 24-year-old artist expresses her deepest passion in writing her first book, *Etched.* She is intuitive and creative. She has always considered writing to be her purpose. Determined to accomplish anything she sets her mind to; this collection of poetry was inspired when she turned to writing as an outlet to express her emotions. Her empathetic nature helped her write poetry that others can relate to. She spends her free time singing and painting. She also loves coffee, nature, and comedies. You can connect with her on Facebook at https://www.facebook.com/profile.php?id=1000 86172006629 and on Instagram at https://www.instagram.com/lf.inspire.writing/

Made in the USA
Columbia, SC
28 October 2022